THiMBLe
MONKEY SUPERSTAR

Jon Blake lives in Cardiff with his partner and two young children. He qualified as a teacher in 1979. His first story was published in 1984; since then he has earned his living as a writer of books, TV and radio scripts, and as a teacher of creative writing. Previous books include the best-selling *You're a Hero, Daley B!*, *Stinky Finger's House of Fun* and *The Last Free Cat*.

Martin Chatterton's own books include *Monster and Chips* (OUP) and some of the *Middle School* books with James Patterson, and he has illustrated many, many books in UK and Australia, including stories by Julia Donaldson and Tony Bradman.

THIMBLE
MONKEY SUPERSTAR

JON BLAKE

ILLUSTRATED BY
MARTIN CHATTERTON

Firefly

First published in 2016
by Firefly Press
25 Gabalfa Road, Llandaff North,
Cardiff, CF14 2JJ
www.fireflypress.co.uk

A CIP catalogue record of this book
is available from the British Library.

ISBN 9781910080344
ebook ISBN 9781910080351

*This book has been published with the support
of the Welsh Books Council.*

Design by: Claire Brisley
Printed and bound by: PULSIO SARL

CONTENTS

DAWSON CASTLE

RED TOWER
Kitchen
JAMS' ROOM
DUNGEON
Moat
CASTLE GROUNDS
Portcullis

CHAPTER ONE

IN WHICH A SO-CALLED HAMSTER FORCES DAD TO DO YOGA

My name is Jams Cogan. You won't have heard of me. But everyone will hear of me one day, because I am going to be the world's greatest author.

My dad is an author. His name is Douglas Dawson. No, he doesn't have the same name as me, because he is not married to my mum. Mum is wise not to be married to Dad, because he has about 20p and lives in a fantasy world. Mum has a proper job, a job which involves going out in the morning, coming back at teatime, and getting paid a lot more than Dad. Dad is always asking her what she actually does, but she's a bit vague about it – it's something to do with the wind, or a farm, or possibly a combination of the two.

Our home is called Dawson Castle. It's not actually a castle. Most people would call it a bungalow. But most people do not live in a fantasy world like my dad.

Not many people visit Dawson Castle. Most are put off by the moat, portcullis, dancing bears and other figments of my dad's imagination. So imagine our surprise one evening when there was a knock at the door.

'Not the Jehovah's Witnesses again!' grumbled Dad.

'When did the Jehovah's Witnesses ever visit?' asked Mum.

'Five years ago. I made a note in my diary.'

'Haven't you got better things to write

about?' asked Mum.

'Not really.'

'Shall I get it?' I suggested.

I got up, seized my walker, and hurried to the West Door at full speed. Imagine my surprise to discover our neighbours standing outside. Nothing unusual about that, you might think, except our neighbours had lived next door my entire life, and had never once spoken to us. But there they were, as clear as day, wearing forced smiles and accompanied by a small, neatly dressed monkey.

'I wonder if you could do us a great favour and look after our hamster while we are away?' enquired the female neighbour, who was not interesting enough to describe in detail.

By now Dad had arrived at the door. He

adopted his most unwelcoming face.

'We'd need to see this hamster,' he replied,

hoping to stall them while he plucked up

the courage to say no.

'Why, it's right here,' said the male neighbour, who looked vaguely like the female. He pointed at the monkey.

Dad's eyes narrowed. 'Are you sure that's a hamster?'

'Oh yes,' they both replied, rather quickly, in fact slightly before Dad had finished the question.

'It looks like a monkey to me,' Dad said.

'It's funny you should say that,' said the man.

'Why?'

'No reason,' replied the man. 'It's just funny.'

As if to show how funny, they both laughed. I may have been mistaken, but I had the distinct impression that there was a third snigger, coming from the direction of the monkey.

This was surely the time to send our two neighbours packing. But no, Dad was too polite for this.

'Is the hamster well behaved?' he asked, making it very plain he did not for one moment believe it to be a hamster.

'Ninety per cent of the time, yes,' replied the woman.

'What about the other ten per cent?'

Suddenly the man pointed dramatically upwards. 'Good heavens!' he cried. 'Isn't that a UFO?'

Dad and I looked at the sky.

'There's nothing…' I began, but when I looked back, my two neighbours, and their so-called hamster, had vanished into thin air.

'Nutters,' grumbled Dad. 'Wind down the portcullis, Jams, just in case they come back.'

I ignored him, as usual, and we went back to the Great Hall for a cup of Horlicks.

'You'll never believe what's just happened,' Dad said to Mum.

'Has it really happened,' asked Mum, wearily, 'or is it something you've made up?'

'It does sound like something I've made up,' Dad agreed, 'but despite that, it really is real.'

'Go on,' said Mum, even more wearily.

'Well,' said Dad, 'our two neighbours came round, and asked if I'd look after their hamster, but – here's the bit you probably won't believe – it was actually a monkey.'

'What, like that monkey?' Mum pointed at the armchair by the fire – Dad's armchair – where, much to our surprise, the said monkey was sitting.

'It's like that story you wrote,' Mum said. 'You know, where the girl finds a cat in her garden, and brings it in, and…'

'Nora, this is not a cat,' Dad snapped. 'It's a monkey. And it's sitting in my chair.'

'It's kind of cute,' observed Mum.

'Cute?' rasped Dad. 'It's plain ugly!'

'It's better looking than you,' said Mum.

'Well, why don't you marry it then?' Dad snapped. It was a stupid and dangerous thing to say. Mum had a habit of doing things just to annoy Dad, and there was a small but distinct possibility this could include marrying an animal.

'We don't even know if we can house-train a monkey,' said Dad, lamely.

'I think it'll be fun,' countered Mum.

'We could do with some fun,' I added.

'We have fun all the time!' Dad protested.

'Name the last time we had fun,' said Mum.

'Last Thursday! Remember, we played Scrabble, and I made a seven-letter word!'

Mum shook her head sadly, as if she felt sorry for Dad, or maybe for herself.

'I'm going up to my office,' said Dad. 'When I come back, I want that monkey gone!'

Dad's office is in the Red Tower. Most people, people without imagination, would call it an attic. Dad has a bed in the Red Tower, an antique captain's chair, a computer, and a window which looks out over the grounds of Dawson Castle, which people without imagination might call a backyard. Dad likes to sit and stare at the computer, sometimes for hours, often without actually switching it on. Sometimes, when his eyes have glazed over, I switch it on myself and write a few stories. If Dad looks particularly depressed I tell him he wrote one of the stories himself, just to see a weak smile come to his face.

This particular evening, Dad ignored the computer and paced the Red Tower, muttering. I sat and looked thoughtful, which seemed the safest thing to do. An hour ticked by, although, strictly speaking, as my watch is digital, an hour went by completely silently. Then Dad and I went back downstairs.

Nothing could have prepared us for the sight which greeted us. Mum sat at the far end of the Great Hall, eyes closed, very still, in a half lotus position. The monkey sat a couple of metres away, facing her, in exactly the same pose.

'What on Earth are you doing?' asked Dad.

'Yoga,' replied Mum.

'With a monkey?'

'Why not?'

'You can't do yoga with a monkey!' declared Dad.

'He's very bendy,' said Mum.

'He's a monkey!' cried Dad. 'Of course he's bendy!'

'And he listens when I talk.'

'He's just trying to get round you!'

'Stop being so jealous,' said Mum.

'Jealous!' snorted Dad. 'Of a monkey?'

'Just because you can't do a half lotus.'

'We'll see about that!' Dad stormed into the centre of the room, cast off his cardigan, and began lowering himself into

a seated position on the floor.

'Dad!' I warned. 'You know what happened last time you…'

'AAAAAAAAARRRRGH!' screamed Dad.

'Oh dear,' I sighed.

'Call 999!' cried Dad.

The monkey reached for the phone.

'Not you!' yelled Dad. 'Nora, call 999!'

Mum wearily rang for an ambulance. 'By the way, Douglas,' she said. 'I've got quiz night tonight. You'll have to take Jams with you to hospital. And Thimble.'

'Thimble?' Dad blurted. 'Who's Thimble?'

'The monkey.'

'Why did you call him Thimble?'

'It's his name.'

'How do you know?'

'He told me.'

'How did he tell you?'

'Sign language.'

'He's not done any sign language to me.'

'You should try being nice to him.'

As Dad was reflecting on this, the
ambulance arrived. Dad sat on one side,
wincing with pain, and Thimble and I sat
on the other, a bit like the opposing team.
It seemed like a great adventure, and unlike

Dad, I was starting to enjoy having a new and unpredictable companion.

CHAPTER TWO

IN WHICH THIMBLE TRAPS A HEFFALUMP IN A DEAD DOG'S KENNEL

I love hospitals. They have ramps and lifts and great long corridors with smooth shiny floors. I can bomb down the corridors in my walker like a Japanese bullet train. My walker's like a frame on wheels, by the way. I can run without it, just not as fast. Once I couldn't run at all, then I had an operation to snip my tendons so I wasn't on tiptoes. I was in a wheelchair for a while, then I recovered, and kazam! I could beat Dad! That's another reason I love hospitals.

Dad hates hospitals. He thinks the lights

are too bright and the waiting areas too clogged up with sick people. That means he has to wait for ages, reading the posters about various illnesses and imagining he's got them all.

And now, on top of this, Dad had Thimble to deal with. Normally, of course, animals are not allowed in hospitals, but Dad had managed to convince the receptionist that Thimble was actually his second son, who had a rare hairy face disorder. Fortunately nurses have seen everything and are therefore prepared to believe almost anything.

Luckily, Thimble was being quite calm and peaceful, possibly because of the yoga. Dad, on the other hand, was shuffling and shifting and moaning and groaning, until I just had to say something to shut him up.

'Why don't we go down to the children's wards after, Dad?' I suggested.

'Children?' grumbled Dad. 'Why on earth would I want to see children?'

'You're a children's author,' I reminded him.

'So?'

'You could do autographs and cheer them up.'

A glimmer of light came to Dad's eyes. 'Hmm,' he said. 'That's not a bad idea. Their mums and dads might buy my books.'

'Yes. Although that wouldn't be the main reason you'd be doing it, would it?'

'Er...' said Dad.

Dad hobbled over to the nearest nurse and explained our plan to him. The nurse put it to a senior staff nurse, who put it to a ward manager, who put it to a senior ward manager, who came up to Dad with a look on her face which was the opposite of trusting. I piped up and explained just how famous Dad was and eventually she caved in. Dad would be allowed half an hour in the children's ward just as soon as he'd had his spine reattached to his legs.

'Excellent idea, Jams,' he said. 'It's good to feel someone again.'

I glowed with pride. It was great to see Dad looking happy for once. He looked even happier after he'd seen the doctor and was no longer bent double like a wall bracket.

'Showtime!' he declared. 'Where's Thimble?'

I glanced around. 'Er...'

'Jams!' barked Dad. 'You were supposed to be looking after Thimble!'

'I was looking after him!' I protested. 'He must have gone while I was sneezing!'

'I'll sneeze you!' rasped Dad. It's just the kind of thing parents say, and doesn't have to mean anything.

'He can't be far,' I said, unconvincingly.

'Do you realise how big this hospital is?' ranted Dad. 'He could be anywhere! He could be in an operating theatre, for heaven's sake!'

I pictured Thimble in a green gown and hat, scalpel in his hairy hand. It was kind of funny, and kind of not funny.

'I'll find him,' I said, but Dad held me back. A new look had come into his eyes, not a particularly nice one.

'Hold your horses, son,' he said. 'I can't be late for my engagement at the children's ward. Thimble will just have to find his own

way home.'

'But Thimble will never find his way home!' I protested.

'He made his bed,' said Dad. 'Now he must lie on it.'

'Er?'

There was no time for explanations. Dad was already striding purposefully towards the children's wards, ferreting in his pocket for his best autograph-signing pen.

'But, Dad!' I cried. 'We can't just abandon him!'

My words fell on deaf ears. Dad was hunting down those sick kids like a heat-seeking missile. We passed the Caring Owl Daycare Centre and the Unity Sheep Sleep Unit. Then, just as we were about to throw open the doors to the children's wards, Dad stopped dead.

There was an unexpected sound coming from the other side of those doors.

Laughter.

'Do you think they're reading one of your books, Dad?' I asked.

Dad seized on this idea. 'Yes, of course. The nurses are obviously preparing them for my visit.'

Dad rubbed his hands vigorously in some antiseptic gel, took a deep breath, and whammed open the doors. 'Good evening, children!' he cried. 'I am Douglas Dawson, the famous...'

He got no further.

All of the children were out of their beds, looking wildly excited, while a hospital trolley raced this way and that down the ward. Behind this trolley, occasionally doing handstands on top of it while tooting a kazoo, was none other than our new hairy housemate.

'Thimble!' I cried.

Dad fixed me with a fierce stare. 'What on earth...' he muttered, as Thimble vaulted

onto an overhanging beam, swung round it
five or six times, dropped onto the nearest
bed, bounced, landed in the toy area and
began juggling with a bunch of plastic balls.

'Maybe he's a circus monkey,' I suggested.

'This is not a circus,' growled Dad. 'This is

a serious building full of sick people.'

'More!' cried the nurses. They were enjoying the show as much as the children.

Dad cleared his throat loudly. 'Excuse me,' he said, 'I have an appointment to sign autographs for these children.'

The nurses did not seem impressed. 'But they're having so much fun,' said one.

'We don't want to spoil it,' said another.

'I'll put it to the vote,' declared Dad. He called for silence and took centre stage. 'Now listen here, children,' he announced. 'We're going to have a vote. You can decide whether you want an autograph from the famous writer, Douglas Dawson – that's me – or some more stupid tricks from the silly monkey. Jams, you count the votes. OK, hands up who wants more stupid tricks from the silly monkey?'

A forest of hands shot up. Dad glowered impatiently as I began counting.

'And who wants..?' he began.

'Hang on, Dad,' I interrupted. 'I haven't finished counting yet.'

'Come on, come on.'

'Fifty-six, Dad,' I declared. 'Or it may be fifty-seven, because I think the boy with the broken arm was trying to lift it.'

'Fifty-six, that'll do,' grunted Dad. 'Now, who wants a fantastic autograph from the world-famous writer, Douglas Dawson?'

No hands.

'Nil, Dad,' I informed him.

'I think I saw a few at the back.'

'No, Dad. Definitely nil.'

'Can the monkey get on with the show now?' asked one of the nurses.

'No,' snapped Dad. 'The monkey's show is

over. It is past the monkey's bedtime.' Quite pink around the ears, Dad rounded on the children. 'Now listen here, you lot,' he growled. 'You play too many video games and watch too much telly and obviously don't read enough books. That is why you are growing up to be losers.'

Dad seized Thimble with one hand and me with the other. We headed for the exit doors in an atmosphere as bleak as Pluto.

'Come back soon!' said a little voice.

'I'll have to check my diary,' grunted Dad.

'Not you,' said the voice. 'The monkey.'

It was quite late when we got home. Mum was already on her way to bed.

'How's Thimble?' she asked.

'Thimble is fine, thank you,' snapped Dad. 'Don't bother asking about my injury.'

'OK. Now, where is Thimble going to sleep?'

'He can sleep on the floor here.' Dad pointed at the grand flagstones of the Great Hall.

'You can't put him there,' said Mum. 'He's in a strange home and he might panic.'

'He can sleep in my room,' I suggested.

'Out of the question,' said Dad.

'Why doesn't he sleep in the attic?' asked Mum.

'The what?' snapped Dad.

'Why doesn't he sleep in the Red Tower?' asked Mum, with a wink to me.

'Because I am sleeping in the Red Tower,' Dad replied.

'You could put an air bed on the floor.'

I could sense an argument brewing, but to my surprise, it didn't come. A fishy look

came onto Dad's face, a look which told me
he was planning something.

'OK,' he said. 'And by the way, why don't
you put some earplugs in, in case he makes
noise in the night?'

'Good idea,' said Mum.

Dad smiled a small, self-satisfied smile
as Mum retired for the night. 'Now, Jams,'
he said, 'you are to go to bed, and whatever
you hear, you are not to get up, is that
understood?'

'But, Dad…' I began.

'No buts!' snapped Dad. 'I do not wish
to see your face until breakfast-time! And
if you put so much as a toe outside your
room, you can forget about using the
computer, or that funny thing by the telly,
for a very long time!'

'Yes, Dad,' I mumbled. I was beginning to

fear the worst for poor Thimble, and sure enough, I had hardly shut my bedroom door when I heard a loud monkey-cackle followed by the slamming of the back door. I peeked through my blind to see Dad dragging Thimble into the backyard to the former home of our dear departed Blyton, i.e. the dog kennel.

'It's perfectly dry,' declared Dad.

Thimble put on a rather pathetic face, but Dad was not in the mood for mercy.

'Sleep tight,' he trilled. 'Don't let the bed bugs bite!'

There were probably quite a few bugs in Blyton's old kennel, and heavens knows what else. Thimble looked the saddest sight in the world as Dad disappeared back into the house. I so wanted to help him, but how could I without putting at least ten toes through my bedroom door? I sidled back to bed and tried to think of something else.

Suddenly, there was a chilling noise from outside. Like a cry of fear. There it was again, even more distressed.

My imagination began to take hold. Had a fox got into the grounds? Some kind of wild dog, a wolf even? I hurried back to the blind and looked outside. There was no sign of a dangerous animal – then Dad appeared.

'OK, old boy,' he asked, 'what's the problem?'

Thimble crept out of the kennel and made a strange sign.

'Fox?' suggested Dad. 'Badger?'

Thimble held up three fingers.

'OK,' said Dad. 'Three words.'

Thimble held up two fingers.

'Second word,' said Dad.

Thimble spread his arms wide, which, being a monkey, was very wide indeed.

'Wide,' suggested Dad.

Thimble shook his head.

'Long,' suggested Dad.

Thimble pointed at Dad and put a finger to his nose, indicating that he'd got it. Then he raised one finger.

'First word,' said Dad.

Thimble cupped a hand round his ear.

'Sounds like,' said Dad.

Thimble's hand ducked up and down, rather like someone using a needle and thread.

'Embroidery?' suggested Dad.

Thimble shook his head.

'Sewing?'

Thimble made the gesture for 'shorter'.

'Sew?'

Thimble nodded vigorously, while Dad frowned, trying to imagine the creature he was describing. Thimble held up his second finger and made the gesture for long.

'Long?' said Dad. Thimble nodded.

Thimble raised three fingers.

'Third word,' said Dad.

Thimble pursed his lips and drew air into them.

'Breathe?' suggested Dad.

Thimble shook his head.

'Suck?' suggested Dad.

Thimble made the gesture for 'longer'.

'Sucking?'

Thimble shook his head.

'Sucker.'

Thimble nodded.

Dad recapped. 'Sew … long … sucker.

Sew long sucker. Eh?'

Dad's words were lost to the night as Thimble set off like a bullet, dodging past him and through the back door. Dad still wasn't moving too well, after the gruesome injuries he had suffered at yoga, and it was some time before he reached the door himself, only to discover, to his obvious dismay, that this was not only shut but firmly locked.

'Nora!' he cried, at Mum's bedroom window.

No reply. Mum had obviously remembered to wear her earplugs, just as Dad had recommended.

'Nora!' bellowed Dad. Still no reply. Nothing but the sound of monkey feet pattering up the stairs towards the warm cosy bed in the Red Tower.

'Jams!' cried Dad.

I ducked back behind the blind. I had not forgotten Dad's terrible warning to stay in my room. If he thought he could tempt me to leave it, he was very much mistaken.

And anyway, there was a perfectly dry kennel in the backyard.

CHAPTER THREE
A HAIL OF SHOES AND A CHAIR FIT FOR A CAT

I woke early next morning, because it felt like Christmas, knowing I had a new special friend in the house. No sign of Mum or Dad, so I crept up to the Red Tower where I found Thimble sitting up in Dad's bed eating a banana from the fruit bowl marked DAD'S.

'Come on, Thimble,' I said. 'Let's go and have some proper breakfast.'

I led Thimble to the kitchen where I introduced him to the microwave. 'This is what you cook things in,' I said. 'Now, let's find some food.'

I ferreted in the cupboard and brought

out a bag of porridge oats, a packet of cornflakes, a tin of beans and a tray of eggs. I put some oats in a bowl, poured on some milk and placed the bowl in the microwave.

'Watch closely, Thimble!' I started the microwave. Thimble cocked his head curiously as the microwave hummed and the bowl turned. His eyes opened wide as I removed the now steaming bowl.

'You can eat this if you like,' I told him. 'I'm just going for a wee.'

We have two toilets in Dawson Castle: the throne room (upstairs) and the dungeon. I prefer the dungeon as it contains the word dung, one of my favourites. It also includes the word eon, which means a very, very long time. So it could mean that dung has been there a very, very long time, or that someone takes a very, very long time to make dung. Like me, for instance. If I get my face in a book I come off the toilet with a seat mark like a cattle brand.

Today, however, I had hardly read the front cover of *Chockoman Returns* when the most almighty KABLAMM filled the house, like a bomb had blown a door off its hinges. If I could have leapt from the toilet I would have done, but I don't move quite as easily as that, and when I did get back into the hallway there was a thick cloud of smoke coming from the kitchen.

'Thimble!' I cried.

Rushing to the kitchen, I found Thimble cowering in the corner, chattering manically. Smoke was billowing from the microwave, the inside of which looked like a mini battlefield.

My eyes scanned the kitchen top: bowl

of porridge … bag of oats … packet of cornflakes … tin of beans…

'Thimble,' I asked, 'where is the tray of eggs?'

Thimble looked furtive.

'Thimble,' I pressed, 'you didn't put the tray of eggs in the microwave, did you?'

Thimble smiled weakly.

Mum burst through the door. 'What on earth is going on?' Her eyes fell on the microwave and she said something else, something quite forceful, something which would not be allowed in a book for children.

'Sorry, Mum,' I blurted, as she opened the microwave door to reveal an apocalypse of eggs.

'Did you do this, Jams?'

'Yes, Mum.' I was scared that if Thimble

did anything wrong, Mum and Dad would get rid of him.

'What in heaven were you thinking?' cried Mum. 'And where is your father?'

As if in reply, there was a frenzied rap on the back door. There stood Dad, or rather a cross between Dad and a hermit crab. His face stuck out of the door of Blyton's old home and the rest of the kennel covered his back like a turtle shell. He did not look happy. When we finally managed to separate him from his night shelter, he gave us a full account of his terrible ordeal, sparing no detail, including the tom cat who decided that Dad's head was part of his territory and marked it accordingly.

'But what were you doing out there?' asked Mum.

'Research,' grunted Dad, who obviously

didn't want to admit he'd been outwitted by a monkey.

'I wish you'd warned me. Then the microwave might not have exploded.'

'Eh?' said Dad.

'Now,' said Mum. 'What is Jams doing today?'

'Woodwork,' replied Dad.

'Not woodwork again,' I groaned.

'Woodwork is a very important skill,' said Dad.

'Shouldn't I do some maths or something?'

'Sounds like a good idea to me,' chirped Mum.

'You're not his teacher,' snapped Dad.

At this point I need to explain something. I do not go to school. Dad thinks he can teach me much better than any teacher, and besides, you can pick up all kinds of bad influences and filthy parasites at school, according to Dad. You can also pick up friends, of course, but Dad doesn't think that's important. Dad has managed perfectly well all his life without friends, apart from the fact he is totally miserable.

'How about if I help you with your writing?' I suggested.

'I don't need help.'

'Excuse me,' I replied, 'but I've read the first chapter of *Pixie Pony Ballerina*, and I think you do.'

'Does everyone here think I'm a complete idiot?' asked Dad.

Mum hummed a little tune and I looked at my shoes.

It was probably a mistake to mention *Pixie Pony Ballerina*. The *Pixie Pony* series had sold about twelvety million, unlike Dad's books, so Dad's publishers had suggested he might like to write one. Dad reluctantly agreed. However, the publishers had already rejected his first offering, *Pixie Pony Accidentally Strays into a Space Rocket and Gets Blasted out of the Earth's Orbit Forever*. Since then Dad had lost heart and run out of ideas. I had loads of ideas, if only Dad would listen to them.

'You'll find some wood in the storehouse and tools in the Bob the Builder cabinet,' growled Dad. 'You can start by making a shelf.'

'Not a shelf again, Dad!'

'With bevelled edges this time.'

My heart sank. 'Can Thimble make one too?'

Dad made no reply. Since he'd appeared

at the back door, he hadn't so much as looked at Thimble. Mum, however, thought it would be a very good idea if Thimble joined in, and as she'd paid for the wood, Dad couldn't argue. Mum went off to work, Dad went out to buy a paper, and my new friend and I collected the wood and opened the Bob the Builder cabinet.

Thimble seemed quite excited at the sight of the tools, and when I took out a saw and began cutting through a plank, his eyes opened as wide as saucers.

'Would you like a go, Thimble?'

Thimble seized the saw with eager hands. He proved to be surprisingly expert at cutting wood. It wasn't long before he had sawn his way through five planks and was looking hungrily for more.

'Don't you think we should bevel the

edges before cutting any more shelves?' I
suggested.

Thimble shook his head vigorously.

'OK,' I said. 'I'll go to the storehouse for
some more wood while you brush up the
sawdust.' I handed Thimble a dustpan and
brush, which he viewed with a distinct
lack of interest. I was not entirely surprised
when the sawdust was still there upon my
return.

Of Thimble, however, or the saw, there was no sign.

'Thimble?'

I went through to the Great Hall. Still no sign of Thimble. I dropped the wood onto the Round Table and sat down to get my breath back.

That's funny, I thought. The Round Table never rested on my knees before. Had my chair got higher?

Or had the table got lower?

'Thimble!' I cried.

No reply. But wait… Wasn't that the sound of sawing, coming from the Red Tower?

No-o-o-o-o-o-o-o-o-o!

At this point Dad arrived home.

'Done your shelves?' he asked.

I nodded nervously.

'Where's the monkey?' he asked.

I shrugged. Dad went to lay his paper on the table and stopped. His face became confused. When he finally put his paper down, it was with a slow, deliberate movement, followed by a curious examination, first of the table, then of me.

'Have you done something to this table?' he asked.

'What kind of thing?'

'I feel … bigger,' said Dad.

'I think maybe you are.'

'How can I be bigger?'

'New shoes?' I suggested.

Dad cocked his head. 'What's that noise?'

'What noise?' I asked.

'Sounds like … sawing,' said Dad.

'Bees?' I suggested.

'Has the monkey got the saw?' asked Dad,

with a look of alarm.

'Er...' I replied.

'For Pete's sake!' cried Dad. 'Where is he?'

'Um...'

Dad rushed from the room, only to
fall over a pair of stools. 'What the...?' he
began. 'Where did they come from?'

I remembered the two tall barstools that
used to stand in roughly the same place.
Yes, we were definitely on the right trail.

'That sawing noise!' cried Dad. 'It's
coming from my room!'

Dad thundered up the stairs, me in hot
pursuit. We arrived at the Red Tower just
in time to see Thimble sever the last leg of
Dad's bed and send it crashing to the floor.

'You... you...' began Dad, but he didn't go
any closer. Thankfully he had realised that
we were unarmed and Thimble had a very

sharp saw.

'Thimble,' Dad said, in a calmer voice, 'hand me that saw.'

Thimble made no move.

'Thimble,' Dad warned, 'it's not a game, now be a good monkey and hand me that saw.'

Thimble stood his ground.

'Thimble, give me the saw!' Dad yelled, leaping towards him with what he hoped was terrifying fury.

With a neat sidestep, Thimble was past both of us and through the door. We chased after him, but with a lightning turn he shot through Dad's legs, back into the Red Tower, slamming and bolting the door behind him.

For a moment, silence. Then the sinister sound of steady sawing.

'My … my...' Dad was lost for words.

'Antique captain's chair?' I suggested.

'Thimble!' cried Dad. 'If you don't open this door...'

His words, needless to say, fell on deaf ears.

'We need a battering ram!' said Dad.

'What about the microwave?' I suggested.

'The microwave?'

'It's heavy. And already broken.'

In truth I didn't know if the microwave was completely broken, but by the time Dad had taken up my suggestion and smashed the door with it, we could safely say it would not be heating up any more porridge. Half a dozen more smashes and the door gave way, revealing a captain's chair now more fitted to a ship's cat. To add insult to injury, Thimble looked most pleased with his work.

'I'll kill you!' cried Dad, but once again Thimble dodged past him and scampered down the stairs, still grasping the saw. Dad gave chase, murder in mind, and I chased Dad, desperate to stop him. We were both met by a hail of shoes, books, vases and cabinets as the manic monkey fled for his life, cackling. He got as far as the Great Hall, where Dad cornered him behind an armchair.

'There's no escape this time, you demon!' rasped Dad.

Dad had clearly underestimated Thimble, who leapt onto the top of the chair, up to the nearest chandelier, then across to the next one.

'Better leave him for a bit, Dad,' I suggested.

'Ha!' said Dad. 'Didn't you know I was a gymnast in my youth?'

'You're not in your youth now, Dad,' I warned.

'The rings were my speciality,' said Dad, climbing onto the armchair.

'Dad! Aren't you a bit big for..?'

Too late. Dad leapt like a very fat gazelle. To my amazement, he made the chandelier. Unfortunately, the chandelier, light cable, ceiling rose and a fair portion of the ceiling then plummeted to the ground with an almighty crash, Dad somewhere beneath it.

'Are you OK, Dad?'

'Must … ring … hospital,' he mumbled. He scrabbled in his pocket, only to realise that the force of the fall had sent his mobile flying halfway across the room.

'Jams,' he muttered. Too late. Thimble

was already down from the chandelier and lolloping towards it. Soon he was sitting a short distance away from us, saw in one hand, mobile in the other.

'Thimble,' groaned Dad. 'Please...'

Seemingly happy with his little victory, Thimble crept over to Dad, and handed him the saw.

CHAPTER FOUR
MEN THAT LOOK LIKE HIPPOS AND SOMETHING LETHAL ON DAD'S FACE

Dad didn't much enjoy his second trip to the hospital, or having to hide every saw in the house, or getting a telling-off from Mum for wrecking the microwave. According to Mum, it was also Dad's fault the furniture got pruned, as he had not properly supervised Thimble. Thimble was not really naughty, just a monkey who acted on instinct, who needed to be taught – patiently – how to behave.

Dad, however, was getting less patient by the hour. As soon as Mum had left for work the next day, he informed me that school was off for the day. We were going on a field trip to the zoo.

'Is Thimble coming?' I asked.

'Oh, yes.'

'Careful, Dad!' I joked. 'They might try to put him in a cage!'

Dad laughed gently.

We didn't tell Thimble where we were going. Dad said he wanted it to be a nice surprise. However, Thimble seemed unusually nervous. As we passed the sign saying 'Cheerful Captives Zoo', he began to whimper rather pathetically. It was almost as if he could read, but that of course would be ridiculous. No monkeys can read, and not many children either, judging by Dad's book sales.

The smart young man at the pay desk looked almost as worried as Thimble. He obviously wasn't used to seeing monkeys queuing up to come in.

'Good morning!' said Dad, brightly. 'May I see the zoo manager?'

With a suspicious eye on both Dad and Thimble, the smart young man got on the phone.

'Why are we seeing the zoo manager?' I asked.

'It's part of your education.'

The zoo manager was an older man with a beard, which made him look ever-so-slightly like a monkey himself. They say if you live with a dog long enough you grow to look like it, so maybe a similar thing happens to zoo managers and their animals. There were probably other people at the zoo who looked like aardvarks and hippos.

Anyway, Dad engaged him in a bit of
small talk, except Dad isn't much good at
small talk, so he moved quickly on to some
bigger talk and finally the whopping great
talk he had clearly been planning all along.

'My monkey would like to join your zoo,'
he declared.

'What?' I cried. 'No, he wouldn't!'

Ignoring my protests, Dad explained that Thimble had been pining for other monkeys, and how we didn't want any money for him, just a little plaque with Dad's name on it and the address of his website.

'Hmm,' replied the zoo manager. 'We are actually looking for a monkey. What species is he?'

'Um...' dithered Dad. 'A naughty monkey?'

The zoo manager frowned. 'A naughty monkey,' he said, 'is not a breed.'

Dad thought again. 'It's a long shot,' he began, 'but is it possible he's a hamster?'

'What?' said the zoo manager.

'Hamster monkey, I mean,' blabbed Dad, desperately trying to save face.

'That,' replied the zoo manager, 'is something of which I've never heard.'

'No.' Dad was getting very pink around the ears. 'They're very rare. Nice grammar, by the way. Most people would have said "something I've never heard of". I'm a writer, by the way.'

The zoo manager checked his watch.

'So how come you're looking for a monkey?' asked Dad, trying to change the subject.

'We've had a death,' replied the zoo manager.

Thimble, who had been surprisingly quiet up till now, began to whimper again.

'Bad luck,' said Dad.

'It's very sad, seeing the empty cage,' murmured the zoo manager.

'Have you ... been in it?' asked Dad. It

was a really stupid thing to say, especially with the zoo manager looking a bit like a monkey.

The zoo manager did not reply. His eyes were resting on Thimble, whose own eyes were dashing from side to side looking for an exit.

'Lovely little feller,' mused the zoo manager.

'Oh, yes,' replied Dad. 'And very well behaved.'

'Apart from sawing up our furniture and blowing up the microwave,' I added.

Dad laughed. 'My son lives in a fantasy world.'

The zoo manager pondered a moment.

'OK,' he said. 'We'll take him.'

My heart sank. Dad beamed. Thimble let out a stream of desperate gibberish. The

zoo manager took us to an empty cage
which still bore the name BOBO above
a picture of the poor departed monkey.
Bobo's favourite tyre was still hanging
inside and his last dollops were still on the
straw.

'Perhaps we could call the new monkey
Bobo Two,' said the zoo manager.

'His name's Thimble,' I grunted.

'Perhaps we could combine the two
names,' suggested the zoo manager. 'That's
it, we'll call him Bobble.'

'Why can't you just call him Thimble?'

'Welcome to your new home, Bobble,'
said the zoo manager, opening the cage
door.

Thimble was not about to go in quietly.
It took the zoo manager and Dad all their
strength to force him through the door.

Once inside, he looked about himself with dismay, then adopted the most pathetic face imaginable, as if pleading with us to spare him.

Dad's heart was as hard as stone.

'Now, about this plaque...' he began.

There followed a tedious discussion about the exact size, colour and position of the plaque. The zoo manager did not seem that keen on the idea, doing all he could to put some distance between himself and Dad, and in the process backing quite close to the bars of Thimble's cage. A large ring of keys hung from his belt, including the key which had just locked the cage. Not surprisingly, Thimble was taking an interest in these keys, and before long his clever monkey fingers were stretching through the bars to grasp them.

Alas, just too far away.

Hmm, I thought. Maybe I could help a little...

'Excuse me,' I said, brightly, 'but would it be possible for me to take a photo as a keepsake?'

The zoo manager leapt at the chance to end his conversation with Dad. 'Of course,' he said. 'Would you like me to move out of the way?'

'No, I'd like you and Dad in it, please,' I replied. 'If you stand by the cage, I can get both you and Thimble in the shot.'

The zoo manager was very obliging. I think sometimes people are more obliging to me because I've got a walker. It makes them think I'm a little angel.

Snigger, snigger.

'Just a bit closer to the cage,' I advised.

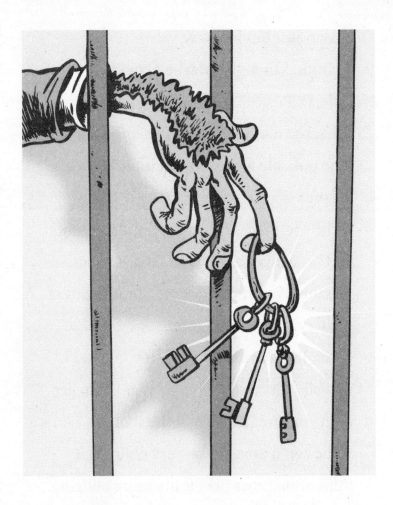

'Should we say Cheese?' asked the zoo manager.

'Whatever,' I replied, as Thimble's skilful fingers released the ring of keys and drew

them into the cage.

'Just a couple more shots,' I said.

A couple of shots was all it took for Thimble to unlock the cage and run for it. It was only now that the zoo manager cottoned on to what was happening.

'The monkey's free!' he cried, reaching for his non-existent key ring. 'And … he's got my keys!'

'How did that happen?' said Dad.

I shrugged.

'He won't do anything silly with those keys, will he?' asked the zoo manager.

'Er...' said Dad.

'For Pete's sake!' cried the zoo manager. 'After him!' He set off with impressive speed, Dad struggling to keep up due to his many injuries and big wobbly gut. By now, however, Thimble was completely out of sight. I watched the zoo manager, then Dad, disappearing round the corner and wondered if I should look a bit more keen to give chase.

Much to my surprise, however, the zoo manager was soon back in sight, running in the opposite direction, yelling at the top of his voice, 'Run for your life! The rhino's out!'

I didn't much fancy my chances of outrunning a rhino, so I ducked behind a

nearby map of the zoo, using my walker as a shield. Dad appeared first, looking amazingly scared. Hearing my yells, he dodged into my hidey-hole to heave for breath. Next up, as promised, came the rhino, not exactly charging, more jogging. It was still a fearsome sight, especially when followed by two giraffes, a giant panda and a small pack of meerkats. Three keepers came next, driving something like a golf buggy and armed with dart guns. It was all

very exciting, the kind of excitement which makes you wish you'd brought a spare pair of pants.

In time, order was restored. The cafe and toilets were a bit of a mess, but the animals were back in their cages. Then, finally, two keepers turned up, with Thimble in handcuffs.

'I believe this is your monkey,' one said.

'Er … is that our monkey?' asked Dad.

'Yes, Dad,' I confirmed.

'We found him in the tropical house,' added the keeper.

'He does like warm places,' said Dad.

'In that case,' replied the keeper, 'make sure the fire's on when you take him home.'

Dad faced Thimble across the refectory table, glowering. 'Do you realise what a stupid and dangerous thing you did today?' he asked.

Thimble nodded eagerly.

'Those animals could have killed us!'

Thimble gave a toothy smile.

'Thank heaven you didn't bring any of them home with you,' added Dad.

Thimble's eyes went from side to side in a decidedly shifty way.

'Thimble,' said Dad, sternly. 'You didn't bring any of them home with you, did you?'

Thimble shot a glance at his shirt pocket.

'Thimble,' Dad said, even more sternly, 'what is in your pocket?'

Thimble's hand rummaged in his pocket, then lowered to the table. There were a few seconds of suspense, then, like a conjuror, he lifted it to reveal...

AIEEEEEEEEE!

A TARANTULA!

If anything, Dad screamed louder than
I did. The noise must have alarmed the
tarantula, which bolted straight towards
him. Before Dad could say Jack Robinson,
which was probably not what he felt
like saying, the eight-legged horror had
scurried up his arm and settled, like a hairy
nightmare, right on his face.

Dad stayed very still. 'Jams,' he whispered.
'Would you be so kind as to hand me the
phone?'

I did as asked, switching on the
speakerphone in case there was anything
that Thimble and I needed to hear. As
calmly as possible, Dad tapped out Mum's

work phone number, and after a few anxious rings, we heard her familiar tones. 'I hope you're not dumping some problem on me,' she said, 'because I've got enough problems of my own.'

'OK,' replied Dad, as calmly as possible. 'You tell me your problem, then I'll tell you mine.'

'We've had a fire in a wind turbine,' said Mum.

'Wow,' replied Dad.

'I wouldn't expect you to understand.'

'Good,' said Dad. 'Now can I tell you my problem?'

'Hurry up then,' said Mum.

'There's a tarantula on my face.'

Silence.

'I wouldn't expect you to understand,' added Dad.

'Are you serious?'

'Oh, yes,' said Dad. 'And so's the tarantula.'

'How did it get there?' asked Mum.

'Up my arm and across my neck.'

'Don't panic. Tarantulas aren't as bad as people think.'

'Try saying that with one on your face.'

'It's probably more scared of you than you are of it,' said Mum.

'I wouldn't bet on it,' replied Dad. 'Do you have any useful suggestions?'

'You can use smoke to make them drowsy,' suggested Mum. 'Or is that bees?'

'You're helping so much.'

'I don't know!' snapped Mum. 'Just knock it off with something!'

'Like what?'

There was no reply. I noticed at this point that Thimble was no longer sitting at the table. No, he was right there beside me, holding a cricket bat, which he offered up to me.

'Dad,' I said, 'look what Thimble's got.'

Dad switched off the phone and, keeping his head very still, examined the bat. Could Dad hit the spider hard enough to kill it, but soft enough not to smash his own face in? A delicate task, but Dad had often told me how brilliant he used to be at cricket.

Keeping his face rock steady, he tried a few practice swings.

'OK, Jams,' he whispered, 'I need you to help me. I need to know exactly when to stop the bat, do you understand? So the very second I make contact with the spider, I want you to shout STOP, do you understand?'

It was a daunting responsibility. 'Can't

Thimble do it?' I asked.

'That,' said Dad, 'would be sheer idiocy.'

'But his reactions are faster than mine.'

'I don't trust him,' said Dad.

'I do.'

'It's not your face,' said Dad.

'I can't do it, Dad.'

'OK! OK!' Dad attempted to compose himself. 'Now listen, Thimble,' he whispered. 'I need to know exactly when to stop the bat, OK? So the very second I make contact with the spider, I want you to make that HOO noise that monkeys make, do you understand?'

Thimble nodded. Dad steadied his arm.

'One...'

'Two...'

'THREE!'

The tarantula bolted.

By now, however, the bat was already on its way, and what a shot it was! If that bat had struck a cricket ball, it would have cleared the ground, let alone the boundary. Unfortunately, however, the bat did not strike a cricket ball. It hit the centre of Dad's face. His proud nose, which had stuck out from his face all his life, suddenly did not stick out any more, and Dad dropped to the floor, rolling around and crying out in some language he had never spoken before.

'Hoo,' said Thimble.

Dad struggled into a sitting position and grabbed a tea towel to staunch the bleeding.

'Did you … see where … the spider … went?' he gasped.

Oh dear. Now we had a tarantula loose in Dawson Castle, a place with so many dark corners it could hide a yak.

CHAPTER FIVE

NITS GALORE AND UNFORGETTABLE SARNIES

Mum did not ask about the tarantula when she came home, so Dad said nothing about it and nor did I. Dad was still sulking about their phone conversation, and I was trying to keep Thimble out of trouble. Since I'd helped him escape from the zoo, Thimble had become the bestest best friend I could ever have imagined. He even helped me take my splints off at night and put them back on in the morning. Dad didn't complain about that, since it was one less job for him. He didn't complain about Thimble sleeping in my room, either. Suddenly everything was perfect, but it was against the rules of Dawson Castle for everything to be perfect, so Dad soon had another plan to mess things up.

'I'm taking Thimble to school today,' he declared, next morning.

'Eh?' I said.

'Is that a good idea?' asked Mum.

'It is an excellent idea. The teachers can take care of him while I get on with *Pixie Pony Ballerina*.'

'Teachers don't look after monkeys,' said Mum.

'Where there's a will, there's a way,' replied Dad.

'Please don't ring me if things go wrong,' warned Mum. 'And don't forget I'm going cycling after work. I'll need some sandwiches.'

'You really could do with a servant,' said Dad.

'A helpful partner would be fine,' replied
Mum.

'Tarantula sandwich coming up,' growled
Dad, as the front door shut.

I put an arm round my hairy friend.
'Dad,' I said, 'you're not really taking
Thimble to school, are you?'

Thimble started whimpering horribly,
just like when they were putting him in the
cage.

'School, Thimble, not zoo,' I assured him.
'It's a place with teachers.'

Thimble whimpered again.

'Teachers, Thimble, not keepers,' I said.

'You're not helping,' said Dad.

'That's a funny idea though, isn't it, Dad?
That school is a zoo, and teachers are
keepers? We could write that as a story
later.'

'Right, let's go,' said Dad, not bothering to respond to my great idea. 'Come on, Thimble.'

Thimble seemed to misunderstand this entirely, taking it as an offer of friendship, and bounded across the room to plant himself on Dad's lap. Dad froze. Thimble started enthusiastically picking through Dad's hair.

'What? What on earth are you…?' Dad began, but his words dried as Thimble discovered something in Dad's hair, which he happily popped into his mouth.

'He's found a nit!' I cried.

'There are no nits in my hair!'

But Thimble was on fire now, popping little somethings into his mouth like peanuts.

'He's grooming you, Dad,' I declared. 'It's a

sign of submission.'

'I do not wish to be groomed!' barked
Dad. 'And if he wants to show submission,
he can put on his coat and follow me out of
the front door!'

It was a strange feeling to be standing

at the gates of Peterloo Primary, looking into its playground of trees, colourful murals and climbing frames. This was the place Dad swore I would never go to. Who knows how many friends I might have found there?

Dad pressed the intercom button and a voice said, 'Hello?'

'It's Douglas Dawson,' said Dad.

Silence.

'The famous author,' added Dad.

Hushed voices. I couldn't be quite sure what they said, but it sounded like, 'It's him again.' A louder voice said, 'As I have repeatedly told you, Mr Dawson, we don't have funds for an author visit this year.'

'It's not about that,' snapped Dad. 'I've come to enrol my son.'

What?

'You'd better come in,' said the voice.

Mrs Timms had probably seen everything, being a headteacher, but she did not look entirely comfortable having a monkey in her room. She moved her mug and books well out of his reach and kept an anxious eye on him as she addressed me and Dad.

'So,' she said, 'you've had a change of heart.'

'Not entirely,' said Dad.

'But you want your son to enrol?' said Mrs Timms.

'Did I say "my son"?' asked Dad. 'I'm sorry, that was a slip of the tongue. I meant the monkey.'

This was a horrible disappointment to me, and even more to Mrs Timms. 'The monkey?' she repeated.

'He's very mature for his age,' Dad assured her.

'His maturity,' declared Mrs Timms, 'is not the issue.'

'I see,' said Dad, bristling. 'And what exactly is the issue?'

'The fact he is a monkey!'

Dad was obviously well prepared for this reaction. 'I see,' he countered. 'And can you quote me the law which says schools must only teach humans?'

'Of course we only teach humans!' protested Mrs Timms.

'I have studied all the Education Acts,' replied Dad, 'and I cannot find one which says school is not for monkeys.'

Mrs Timms was thrown for a moment, but came back strongly. 'How are we supposed to teach him how to read?' she asked.

'He already can read! Thimble, pick up a book and show Mrs Timms how you can read.'

Thimble picked up a copy of *Whiteboards for Dummies*, opened it and began looking at it quite intelligently.

'See?' Dad said. 'He's reading.'

'The book is upside down,' said Mrs Timms.

'That's the way monkeys read. You know, like people in China read backwards.'

Mrs Timms was not impressed. 'Think of the health risks.'

'What health risks?' asked Dad.

'I can't imagine what fleas and ticks he's carrying,' she replied. 'We've already got a head lice outbreak in year one.'

Dad's eyes lit up. 'A head lice outbreak?'

'I send letters home, but I'm sure parents

never read them,' complained Mrs Timms.

Dad rose dramatically. 'Mrs Timms,' he declared, 'your head lice problems are over.'

'How is that?'

'May I present Thimble,' proclaimed Dad, 'the best nit nurse you'll ever find.' And before Mrs Timms could protest, off he went down the corridor, Thimble in hand, in search of the year one classroom. By the time Mrs Timms and I arrived, Thimble and Dad had already found their prey, who stared in goggle-eyed delight at the real live monkey in their midst.

'Who's got nits?' demanded Dad.

'It's a monkey!' cried a little girl.

'Top of the class,' said Dad. 'Take a seat.'

Before Mrs Timms or the class teacher could protest, the little girl took the chair Dad had offered and Thimble was sorting through her hair like a monkey possessed. One, two, three tasty morsels disappeared down Thimble's gullet. Hands shot up all round the room and pupils cried out to be next in line. One volunteer followed another to the nitpicking chair, smiles as wide as watermelon slices, and soon even Mrs Timms was beginning to soften.

'I think we can forget about the letters home, Miss Price,' she said.

'He does seem to be doing a good job,' agreed the class teacher.

'I suppose we could have him as a class pet,' suggested Mrs Timms.

'We did have a stick insect last year,' replied the class teacher.

'How do you feel about keeping Thimble, Class One?' asked Mrs Timms.

There was an enormous cheer.

'Very well, Mr Dawson,' said Mrs Timms. 'I'll put his name in the register.'

Dad, needless to say, was delighted. I'd have been delighted too, if I could have

stayed with Thimble. But I dutifully waved him goodbye, which came as a bit of a shock to him. Not that there was long to think about it, with twenty-four more pupils queuing up for grooming.

Dad, at last, was ready for work. *Pixie Pony Ballerina* was up on screen and he was full of inspiration.

'A full day to write, and no monkey!' he purred. 'What luxury!'

'I don't think he wanted to be left on his own,' I said.

'He'll be fine.'

'What am I supposed to do?' I asked.

'Make your mum's sandwiches.'

'That's not schoolwork!' I protested. 'Can't I help you?'

'I,' declared Dad, 'do not need help.'

With that, he rattled feverishly at the keyboard for about two minutes, before grinding to a halt, pondering for about ten minutes, then writing another word or two. His shoulders began to sag. 'Hmm,' he said. 'Perhaps you could just have a look at this for me'.

I studied the screen:

PIXIE PONY BALLERINA – IDEAS

- Pixie Pony loads the dishwasher but it leaks and his hooves get wet.
- Pixie Pony gets magic fairydust on the carpet and has to mend the vacuum cleaner.
- Pixie Pony makes a fish pie but it boils over and makes a big mess in the oven.

'What do you think?' asked Dad. 'Be honest.'

'It's pathetic, Dad.'

'Not that honest,' said Dad.

'You should ask me, Dad, I've got millions of ideas.'

The conversation got no further as the phone rang. 'Yes?' snapped Dad.

'Is that Thimble's parent?' said a voice.

'Why do you ask?'

'You'd better get to school right away,' said the voice. 'Thimble's had an accident.'

My heart went through my boots. I pictured Thimble stone-still in the playground after falling off the school roof. Weak and pale in the medical room, having swallowed a bottle of glue. Grilled to a cinder in the school ovens.

'Come on, Dad!' I cried.

It's fair to say we turned a few heads on our way back to Peterloo Primary. It had been a long time since Dad had run, or even walked fast. His face was lobster red and slobber gushed from his mouth as he blundered up the pavement behind me. Yes, behind me, because my walker was moving faster than a Ferrari.

Thank heaven, my worst fears were not realised. The moment I reached the gate I saw Thimble, conscious, apparently unharmed, but wearing a strange pair of baggy shorts.

'Is he okay?' I gasped.

Mrs Timms, standing stony-faced beside Thimble, held out a bulging plastic bag, tied securely at the top.

'Thimble,' she declared, 'has soiled his pants.'

Dad sat with his head in his hands as far as possible from the Bag of Shame. Thimble

and I sat opposite, Thimble looking quite
happy with the world.

'Why, oh why, oh why?' asked Dad. 'He's
never pooed his pants once at home.'

'Maybe he was distressed, Dad,' I
suggested.

'Distressed? What did he have to be distressed about? He had it made at that school!'

'Maybe he missed us, Dad.'

Dad huffed. 'This is all your fault, Jams,' he declared. 'You've made him needy. You should have kept him at arm's length, like I do.'

'But he's my best friend,' I protested.

'Ha!' said Dad. 'What does that say about you, that your best friend is a monkey?'

'It says I've got one more friend than you,' I replied.

Dad bristled. 'The lone wolf,' he declared, 'is the strongest wolf.'

'Shouldn't that be the saddest wolf?'

Dad was clearly tiring of the conversation.

'Okay, Smartypants,' he replied. 'As you're

Thimble's best friend, you can clean his dirty pants.'

With that, Dad left me to gaze upon the Bag of Shame and wonder what on earth to do with it. I couldn't put Thimble's pants in the washing machine without scraping out the poo, and there was no way I was doing that. Nor could I bury the bag in the castle grounds, because some cat was bound to dig it up, and anyway, Mum would wonder where Thimble's trousers had gone, and I'd have to make up a story, which Mum was bound not to believe, because she never believes my stories any more than she believes Dad's, even though mine have got much longer sentences, like this one.

There was only one answer. I would have to put the bag inside another bag, or even better, a box, then hide it till I could save up enough pocket money to pay someone to get rid of it.

I scoured the kitchens of Dawson Castle. Aha! A cupboard full of plastic storage boxes, one the perfect size. I squeezed the Bag of Shame into this box and secured the lid. No smell. Hallelujah!

At this point Dad called me. 'Where is Thimble?'

'Er … not sure, Dad.'

'I thought I could hear sawing,' said Dad.

'Haven't noticed it,' I replied.

'I'm sure I heard it,' said Dad.

'You may be paranoid.'

'Jams,' replied Dad, 'I'm sitting on an antique captain's chair with two-inch legs. Does that make me paranoid?'

'No, Dad,' I said. 'Just too old to know centimetres.'

'I'm sure I hid all the saws,' said Dad.

'Go through them,' I suggested.

'Hand saw...' began Dad. 'Tenon saw ... panel saw ... coping saw ... mitre saw ... I've got a feeling there's another one, but I just can't think what it is.'

'Cold saw?' I suggested.

'What?'

'You know, the type you get on your mouth.'

Dad viewed me wearily. 'You're not helping.'

'See-saw?' I suggested.

Dad ushered me to the door. 'Maybe you are well suited to having a monkey for a best friend,' he said.

Mum came home in a great mood, possibly because she was going straight out again. There seemed no point in telling her about Thimble's little accident. She put on her cycling gear, and just as she was leaving, gave Dad a peck on the cheek.

'What was that for?' asked Dad, looking surprised and delighted.

'You remembered,' replied Mum.

'Remembered what?'

'To make my sandwiches.'

With that, Mum was gone, leaving Dad baffled. 'Did you make sandwiches for your mother?' he asked me.

'Sorry, I forgot.'

Dad's eyes narrowed. 'Thimble couldn't have made them, could he?'

'Maybe that was the sawing sound,' I suggested.

Equally puzzled, we made our way back to the kitchen. Here I made a disturbing discovery.

The plastic storage box, which I'd left by the fridge, was nowhere to be seen.

'Dad,' I asked, anxiously, 'have you moved a plastic storage box?'

'I haven't seen a plastic storage box.'

'That's strange,' I said.

'Maybe your mum picked it up,' said Dad.

Mum?

Hang on...

NO-O-O-O-O-O-O-O!

'Mum!' I cried, hurrying to the front door.

'Mum, wait!'

Gone!

'What's the matter?' asked Dad.

'The pooey pants!' I gasped. 'Mum's got the pooey pants!'

'What?' said Dad.

'She … thinks they're her … sandwiches!' I blurted.

'What?' cried Dad. 'I'll get the blame for this!'

He rushed back inside Dawson Castle.

'Where are you going, Dad?'

'To get my bike!'

Dad often told me what a great cyclist he'd been back in the day, and here was his chance to prove it. We hurried to the storehouse, where the back wheel of his trusty steed was just visible amongst the junk. Dad and I grabbed the saddle and gave the great beast a yank, only to crash onto our backs as it shot out easier than a knife through butter.

There was a good reason for this. We were holding slightly less than half a bike. It was only now that we saw the rest of the bike, arranged in pieces in a neat pile, and behind that Thimble, holding the hacksaw that Dad had unfortunately forgotten to hide.

CHAPTER SIX
WOW, THIS REALLY IS GETTING TO BE LIKE A PROPER NOVEL

As we know, Dad was familiar with kennels, but now he really was in the doghouse. Mum was barely speaking to him.

'Nora, I keep telling you!' he pleaded. 'Jams put the pants in the sandwich box!'

'Jams would never do such a thing.'

'Tell her, Jams!' demanded Dad.

'What, Dad?' I replied, cunningly. 'The whole story?'

That fixed Dad. Mum would not be pleased to hear about Thimble being taken to a school and left there.

'Anyway,' said Dad, 'I tried to catch you,

except…'

'What was that?' Mum exclaimed, interrupting him.

'What?' asked Dad.

'Something just ran under the fridge,' said Mum.

'It did?'

'I think it was a mouse.'

'Did it have eight legs?' I asked, like an idiot.

'I beg your pardon?' said Mum.

I had to think quickly. 'A while ago I stapled two mice together,' I blustered.

'You did what?'

'No, not stapled,' I blabbed 'What's the word for when you fix two things together with a hair bobble?'

'Jams,' said Mum, sternly, 'you've been spending too much time with your dad.'

'I know, Mum,' I replied.

'Well, how about if you spend more time with Jams?' suggested Dad. 'You could take him to work with you, and, come to that, you could take Thimble too.'

Mum left without even bothering to respond to this idea.

'Maybe we should get Thimble a job,' I said.

'Hmm,' said Dad, thoughtfully.

'It's a joke, Dad,' I explained.

'Let's think,' said Dad. 'What kind of job could a monkey do?'

'No one's going to employ a monkey!'

'There's a night club round the corner,' Dad said. 'They must have dozens of jobs there.'

'Dad,' I pleaded, 'no one wants a monkey DJ.'

'Why not? They could call him the Funkymonkey.'

'Dad, you're losing it!' I said. 'Why don't you just buy him a guitar and call him the Punkymonkey!'

'Do try to be serious, Jams.'

There was no arguing with Dad when he'd got his mind fixed on something.

Twenty minutes later, we were on our way to Jackals Nightclub accompanied by a puzzled-looking Thimble, his hair combed, his teeth brushed and his baggy shorts straightened.

A surprise awaited us. Around the nightclub was a tall plywood fence and a lot of men in hard hats looking busy. Through a gap in the fence we could see bulldozers and excavators. Jackals Night Club was about to be demolished.

'What's the chances of that?' groaned Dad.

'Nice vehicles,' I muttered. In my mind I was climbing into one of those mighty machines, pulling the levers, feeling the power. Maybe I wouldn't be a writer after all. Who wanted to sit at a PC when they could be smashing down a wall?

'Hang on, Dad,' I suggested. 'Why can't Thimble be a demolition worker? He's already demolished half of Dawson Castle.'

'Hmm,' said Dad. 'You have a point there.'

We sought out a big beardy man who seemed to be in charge of things. 'Excuse me,' said Dad. 'Do you have any jobs?'

The beardy man looked Dad up and down. As usual, Dad was wearing his cravat and his Terry Pratchett hat. These showed people that Dad was an Author. Or a nerd. You can guess which the beardy man thought.

'For you?' he asked, dourly.

'For the monkey,' replied Dad.

The man turned his gaze on Thimble. When he looked back there was a strange grin on his face which I could not quite read. 'Let's get this straight,' he said. 'There's ten thousand people looking for work in this town and you want me to give a job to a monkey?'

'He's very good with heights,' said Dad.

'Shaun!' yelled the man. 'Any work for a monkey?'

Another man came over, then a couple of others. Thimble was quite the centre of attention. There was much laughter and a few more of those grins I couldn't quite read. The men took Thimble off and to Dad's great delight put him in the cab of the excavator. The excavator driver let Thimble play with some levers while the others took pictures with their mobiles. It really was a happy scene, but just as we were about to head for home Thimble was brought back down and they all turned to Dad.

'Thanks, mate,' said the beardy man.
'You've made our day. Now, could you get something for me?'

'What's that?' asked Dad.

'Lost,' replied the beardy man. There was much laughter.

'Get … lost?' repeated Dad. 'Oh, I see.'

'Nice hat,' said one of the other men, with a wink to me.

'Thank you,' replied Dad. 'Come along, Thimble, we know when we're not wanted.'

Summoning up as much dignity as possible, Dad took Thimble by the hand and we departed the scene. 'By the way,' Dad called back. 'I'm a famous author. How many books have you written?' It was amazing how brave Dad felt when he wore Terry Pratchett's hat.

Back at Dawson Castle, Dad made a list of other jobs Thimble might apply for. Dad says it is good to make lists, because it feels like you have done something, even if you don't actually do anything. Meanwhile, I searched half-heartedly for the tarantula and Thimble just sat around. He seemed quite miserable, which was not like Thimble at all. I wondered if he was pining for something, a mate maybe, or a tree he used to swing about in.

Time wore on, then on a bit more. I did some dumb odd jobs like putting the rubbish out. More time wore on till it was time for afternoon tea. I thought it might cheer Thimble up to have a custard cream, but when I offered him one he wasn't there. I wandered through the castle calling his name, but no reply. Then I noticed that the portcullis was raised and the front gate left open, possibly by me when I took out the rubbish. Had Thimble left the castle? Why? And where would he have gone?

'Dad!' I cried. 'Thimble's gone a bit missing.'

Dad appeared, looking weary. 'And?' he said.

'And hadn't we better find him?'

'Hmm...' said Dad.

'Well, I'm going to find him!' I grabbed my coat and walker.

Dad followed. He knew how much trouble he'd be in if I got lost. We retraced the steps of our morning walk, in case the hard hats had caught sight of Thimble, who they were sure to remember. When we reached the demolition site, however, everything was shut and there was no sign of any one.

'Must have clocked off for the day,' said Dad.

'Hang on.' I pointed. 'One of the diggers is still moving.'

Dad turned to see a vast yellow excavator looming over the plywood fence like a giant metal giraffe. 'I say!' he yelled, but there was no reply. The driver was busy at his controls. I say 'his' controls, but it was hard to tell at that distance whether it was a man. It could have been a woman, or even a child, because he or she did look rather small. And hairy. Remarkably hairy. Almost like a … a...

NO-O-O-O-O-O-O-O-O-O-O-O!

'Thimble!' I cried. 'Get out of there!'

'What?' yelled Dad.

'It's Thimble, Dad!' I said. 'He's in the…'

The excavator bucket smashed into the nearest wall, sending a cascade of bricks to the ground.

'Good grief!' cried Dad. 'It is Thimble!'

'The power's gone to his head, Dad!' I

cried. 'We've got to stop him!'

Dad put both hands round his mouth and yelled for all he was worth, 'Thimble! Stop that this minute!'

Dad's words were wasted. Thimble was determined to turn the rest of the building to rubble. The excavator arm swung wildly from side to side, bucket crashing into chimneys, walls, windows and doors.

'Thimble!' Dad yelled again. 'Stop this minute or I'll ring the police!'

'Not the police, Dad!' I pleaded, but right then a large portion of roof tumbled to the ground and Dad made good his threat.

'Is it an emergency?' came a dry voice.

'It's a monkey in an excavator,' replied Dad. 'What would you call it?'

'Someone put a monkey in an excavator?' asked the voice.

'No, the monkey got in the excavator of his own accord,' Dad said, 'and now he's demolishing a nightclub.'

There was a short silence. 'A monkey is demolishing a nightclub?' The voice didn't sound at all convinced.

'Yes, now send three cars and an armed response unit, and make it snappy!'

'I must warn you,' came the reply. 'All prank calls are investigated and may result in a prison sentence.'

'This is not a prank call!' snapped Dad. 'Why does nobody believe me? I didn't put the pooey pants in my partner's sandwich box either!'

The line went dead. I was glad about that. I decided to tell Thimble a little white lie.

'Thimble!' I cried. 'The police say if you don't stop, you're going straight to the

monkey tank!' It was something I had
made up, but it seemed to have some effect.
The arm of the excavator stopped moving.
The great mechanical beast swivelled on its
shoes. The track began to move again, in
the direction of the plywood fence.
Hells bells! The mad monkey was coming
straight through!

SMA-A-A-A-A-SH!

Dad and I dived for cover as Thimble
thundered over the remains of the fence
and set off down the middle of the
Dogsbridge Road. Cars swerved onto the
pavement. Pedestrians leapt over garden
walls. Vainly we gave chase, yelling,
'Thimble! Stop!' not that a sound could be
heard over the churning engine and the
grinding tracks.

It was not immediately obvious where

Thimble was heading. He passed the Co-op supermarket and St Winifred's Church Hall. He passed the library, the Goat's Arms, Headers the barbers and Eccles the bakers. There was nowhere else to go except...

No! Not that! Anything but that!

Dad's fumbling fingers pressed redial.

'Is it an emergency?' came a dry voice.

'Yes!' cried Dad. 'The monkey … the one in the excavator … he's heading for the police station!'

'I have warned you once,' said the voice.

SMASH! Thimble's bucket tore a big chunk out of the top floor.

'That's him now,' Dad said, and by way of reply, a line of coppers came flying out of the copshop door, just in time to see the next portion of their station tumbling to the pavement. It wasn't long before the whole building was smashed to smithereens, Thimble was escaping over the rooftops, and Dad was supplying the police with the names of Thimble's owners, our neighbours.

CHAPTER SEVEN
A CRAZY MOBILE AND TWO CRAZY APES

Thimble and I were checking through Dad's emails next day when we came across one from his publishers. It said the final deadline for *Pixie Pony Ballerina* had already passed, and unless they got the story in the next week they were cancelling the contract.

Dad didn't seem too pleased when I told him, especially as Mum was listening. 'I've told you a hundred times,' he said. 'Stay out of my business.'

'And I've told you a thousand times,' I replied. 'Don't exaggerate.'

'That's a very old joke, Jams.'

'I've got lots of better ones,' I replied. 'We could use them in *Pixie Pony Ballerina*.'

'For the millionth time,' rasped Dad, 'I do not need any help.'

Mum's head rose from her muesli. 'How many words do you have to write?'

'Ten thousand,' grunted Dad.

'And how many have you written so far?'

'About seven.'

'Seven thousand?' asked Mum.

'Hmm...' said Dad.

'You've written seven?' said Mum. 'Seven?'

'How can I write with that blasted monkey around?'

'Stop using Thimble as an excuse.'

'Have you seen my antique captain's chair?' snapped Dad. 'I haven't even got anything to sit on, for goodness sake!'

Mum laid down her spoon and viewed Dad in a kind of doctorly way. 'You need to get away for a few days.'

'Chance would be a fine thing,' replied Dad.

'You've got a tent,' said Mum.

'Woh, camping!' I cried. 'Can I come?'

'Hang on, hang on,' said Dad.

'It'd be brilliant, Dad!' I said. 'We could light a fire and eat pizza and tell stories and stuff.'

'Yes,' agreed Mum. 'It might just give you inspiration.'

'Or constipation,' grumbled Dad.

'I'll pay for it,' said Mum.

Dad's eyes narrowed. 'How much?' he asked.

'A couple of hundred should cover it,' said Mum. She took a pile of notes from her purse and laid them on the table. Dad viewed them hungrily.

'OK,' he said. 'I'm going to say yes. But I'm not going to say it because you've offered me money. I just need to show Jams what it takes to be a real man.'

'Yay!' I cried. 'Do you hear that, Thimble! We're going camping!'

'Hang on, hang on,' said Dad.

'Obviously you'll have to take Thimble,' said Mum. 'We can't leave him here unsupervised.'

'I am not sleeping in a tent with that monkey!' cried Dad.

'Nonsense,' replied Mum. 'Going camping with Thimble is exactly what you need to do. It'll be like one of those male bonding weekends.'

'I do not want to be bonded to anything,

thank you,' snapped Dad. 'Least of all a monkey!'

'Ok, I'll keep the money,' said Mum. She reached for the pile of notes, only to find that Dad's hand had moved faster than a frog's tongue to cover them.

Dad doesn't believe in campsites.

Campsites have horrible discos, and games rooms, and TV lounges, and worst of all, other people. Dad says proper camping is camping in the woods, or on a mountain, where you have to make your own toilet, and fire, and entertainment. The very thought of this made me want to make a toilet in my pants, but I had to put on a brave face for Mum. Mum was quite anxious about Dad's rough camping plans.

'Don't forget your phone,' she said.

'It's not working today,' replied Dad.

'Douglas,' said Mum, 'you need a phone that works every day, not just some days.'

'It's a nice colour,' replied Dad.

'You'd better borrow my spare.'

'That's thoughtful of you.'

'I don't want Jams and Thimble to get lost,' said Mum.

'Right,' replied Dad, sourly.

'You'll need the passcode,' noted Mum.

'What's a passcode?' asked Dad.

'My birthday,' replied Mum.

This was all getting a bit much for Dad. He was only just getting used to phones that weren't connected to the wall, and Mum's phone was horribly complicated. She could even take photos with it, and – get this – connect to the internet! Crazy!

A few spots of rain were falling as we reached Tuffety Great Wood, but that didn't bother Thimble. He went straight up the nearest tree, swinging from branch to branch, much to Dad's annoyance. 'He should be down here carrying a knapsack,' he said.

'Carrying a what?' I asked.

'Knapsack.'

'Dad, no one says "knapsack" these days.'

'I do,' replied Dad.

'This is why you need my help,' I said.

Dad did not reply. We moved deeper into the wood. 'Dad,' I began, 'do you think we should leave a trail of beans, like Hansel and Gretel?'

'I know where I'm going.'

I wasn't very confident about this. We'd just passed a fallen-down tree which looked exactly like a fallen-down tree we'd passed ten minutes before. Dad insisted that he'd known these woods since he was a child, but it was a long time since Dad had been a child, and most of the trees he'd known then had probably died.

I was beginning to wish I hadn't brought my walker. My walker was fine on hard dirt paths, but as the rain got heavier so the paths got soggier and boggier. Then Dad abandoned the proper paths altogether. He said he was following the sound of running water, because he was looking for the river, but there was running water everywhere. If only I could have gone up in the trees like Thimble. Thimble was still having a whale of a time, and looked quite disappointed when Dad finally said it was time to stop and make camp.

To give Dad credit, we had found a river. It was quite a scary river, running helter-skelter like it was in a desperate hurry to get somewhere. Thimble was not keen on it at all, and kept making little threatening runs towards it as if he could frighten it away. But Dad was adamant that it gave us all we needed as campers: water for drinking and washing, maybe some fish, and protection from wild animals.

We started putting up the tent on a u-bend, so that the river was on three sides of us. With a fire on the fourth side, we would be completely safe from bears, wolves, and all the other dangerous beasts which only existed in Dad's imagination.

The chances of lighting a fire, however, were looking increasingly remote. The rain was hammering down by the time we got the tent up.

'I want to go home,' I complained.

'Don't snivel,' said Dad.

'But we're just going to get soaked!'

'Now listen here,' said Dad. 'The difference between a man and a monkey is that we have the fortitude to look adversity in the eye.'

'We have four whats?' I said. It was difficult to hear anything with the rain thundering on the roof of the tent.

'You'll feel better with some food inside you,' Dad assured me.

'How are we going to cook food?'

'I'll see about lighting this fire,' said Dad.

I didn't bother to argue. Dad would realise soon enough that it was impossible to light a fire where he'd planned. After a brief scout round, sure enough, he was back.

'Jams,' he said, 'when we put up the tent, wasn't the river on three sides of us?'

'That's right.'

'That's funny,' said Dad. 'Now it seems to be on four.'

'What?' I gasped.

'We seem to be on a kind of … island,' said Dad.

'Dad, I think you'd better ring for help.'

'Hah!' said Dad. 'Your mum would love that!'

'Please, Dad,' I pleaded. 'I'm scared.'

'The rain will probably stop soon,' said Dad.

But the rain did not stop. If anything it got heavier. I was starting to imagine my name in the papers, but not in the way I'd always dreamed of.

'Dad,' I said, 'I really think you should ring for help.'

Dad huffed and took out the phone. 'How does this thing work?' He pressed the on-switch, and up came the words:

SLIDE TO UNLOCK

Dad did as requested.

ENTER PASSCODE

'Passcode?' said Dad.

'Mum's birthday,' I reminded him.

'Right,' said Dad. His finger hovered. 'Er...' said Dad.

'Dad,' I said. 'You do know Mum's birthday?'

'Don't you know it?'

'You're her partner!' I said.

'You're her son!'

'You must know it, Dad!' I said.

'Hang on,' said Dad. 'I've just remembered. It's exactly six months after the day your mum and I first met.'

'What day was that?' I asked.

'Er...' said Dad.

'Think, Dad!'

'Her birthday's in September,' said Dad.

'I'm sure of that.'

'Just go through all the days in September,' I suggested.

'Okay,' said Dad. 'I'll start with the first.'

0109.

UURONG PASSCODE. TRY AGAIN

0209

UURONG PASSCODE. TRY AGAIN

0309

UURONG PASSCODE. TRY AGAIN

0409

PHONE IS DISABLED

'What?' cried Dad. 'Stupid phone!'

'It's you that's stupid, Dad!'

'The phone should know her stupid birthday!' cried Dad. 'It's supposed to be a smartphone!'

'Yes, Dad!' I replied. 'That's why it's not letting you use it, cos it thinks you stole it!'

'How ridiculous!' Dad flung the phone, not caring where, but it went straight at Thimble. Thimble sprang into the air, gibbering madly, as it whacked into his shoulder.

'It was an accident, Thimble!' I cried, but he was well beyond reason. He grabbed the phone, and for a moment I feared he would fling it back at Dad. Instead he stuffed it in his pocket and shot up the only tree on our little island. Before my flabbergasted eyes, he then swung through the branches, across the teeming river, and away out of sight.

My lip quivered.

'Don't cry, for goodness sake,' said Dad.

'He's gone!' I blubbed.

'Man up, Jams,' said Dad.

'I'm a boy!' I blubbed. 'And anyway, Mum

says that if you could cry, you wouldn't be so angry all the time!'

'La la, la la,' replied Dad, covering his ears.

'But,' I continued, 'she says you will cry when she finally plucks up the courage to leave you!'

Dad uncovered his ears. 'Did she really say that?'

'Yes,' I mumbled.

There was a long silence, apart from the hammering of the rain, the rushing of the river and a munching sound which turned out to be Dad devouring a large bar of chocolate.

'Isn't there some for me?' I asked.

'I've got some more in my knapsack,' replied Dad.

'Rucksack.'

Dad found me some chocolate, which
calmed me down a bit, but not that much,
because Thimble was still gone and the
river was still rising.

'I hope Nora doesn't think she's keeping

the castle,' said Dad.

'That will be up to the courts to decide,' I replied, 'but it should be fairly straightforward, once she's had you certified insane.'

'I see,' said Dad. 'And how do you feel about this, Jams?'

'You are a bit bonkers, Dad,' I replied.

Dad thought for a while. 'Out of ten,' he said, 'how many marks would you give me as a father?'

I thought for a while. 'Are you including fractions?'

'What, like nine and a half?' asked Dad.

'Yes,' I replied. 'Without the nine.'

'Thanks.'

'Well, you never listen to me!' I complained. 'I've got loads of ideas for stories, and if you'd just listen, maybe we could write a brilliant book, and then you wouldn't have to write *Pixie Pony Ballerina*!'

Dad turned to face me. A raindrop ran down the centre of his face and dripped off the end of his nose. 'If I let you help me,' he said, 'will you tell your mum you think I'm a great dad?'

'If you promise to be nice to Thimble,' I replied.

'Jams,' said Dad. 'You're not facing reality. Thimble's gone.'

'What do you know about reality?' I blubbed and, as if to remind us what reality was, a gush of freezing cold water ran over our feet. 'Get us out of here!' I cried.

Something seemed to stir in Dad. He jumped up and went to the tree that Thimble had climbed, checking out the footholds, but there was little chance he could climb it, and no chance I could. Realising this, he began barging it like an elephant, possibly hoping to make it fall across the river. But even though Dad was rather fat, he would have struggled to bring down a clothes-pole, let alone a tree.

'Maybe we could swim the river,' I suggested.

'Can you swim?' asked Dad.

'Course I can.'

Dad made no move.

'Can you?' I asked.

'Er...' said Dad.

'We're doomed!' I cried.

As if to echo my despair, a crack of thunder filled the heavens. As this subsided, a new and strangely familiar noise followed. Not rain, nor thunder, but a strange shuckering, buckering sound. What was that above us? A giant dragonfly? A vulture? Or… or…

A helicopter!

Dad and I went mental, waving and screaming like a pair of crazy apes. As if on elastic, the 'copter came down towards us, till we could feel the breeze of the rotor blades like the breath of heaven. A door opened, a man on a winch came down, and next thing I was being clipped into a harness and hoisted into the sky. It was the most thrilling ride ever, but the best was yet to come. As I entered the helicopter, who should I see but my greatest and hairiest friend – the friend who had obviously saved my life.

'Thimble!' I cried, throwing my arms around him. 'I thought I'd never see you again!'

Thimble hugged me back full force and gave me a quick check-over for nits.

'But how did you do it, Thimble?' I asked.

'He's a very clever monkey,' replied the helicopter pilot.

Dad arrived in the cabin. Once he'd got over the shock of seeing Thimble, he looked as pleased as me to be with him, and after smiling and nodding rather stupidly for a while, held out his hand. 'Well done, old boy,' he said.

'Dad,' I said. 'I don't think monkeys shake hands.'

'Ah,' said Dad. 'Well, er...' He patted Thimble on the shoulder. 'Good going, Thimbs,' he said.

'Thimbs?' I repeated.

'It's my pet name for him.'

'Since when?' I asked.

'Since now,' said Dad.

'If it's a pet name,' I said, 'he must be our pet!'

'Of course he's our pet,' replied Dad. 'Have I ever suggested he wasn't?'

EPILOGUE
(THAT'S THE END BIT)

We certainly had a busy time once we got back to Dawson Castle. Thimble had a great pile of wooden boxes to saw up for firewood, while Dad and I had five chapters of *Monkeys Over Dover* to write. *Monkeys Over Dover* was the story we thought up on the journey home, or rather I thought up, while Dad explained how important it was to have his name on the cover.

'Mum was right,' I said. 'You just needed to get away.'

'I guess so,' replied Dad. 'There's nothing like nearly dying to get the creative juices flowing.'

Mum arrived home at the usual time. She

was not surprised to see us back so soon, but most impressed to see us all sitting together on the sofa.

'Fantastic,' she said. 'You've bonded.'

'Yes, Mum,' I replied, 'and guess what, me and Dad are writing a book together, and it's all about Thimble and all his mates, and they've all got helicopters, and...'

Dad gave me a dig in the ribs.

'Oh yes,' I said, 'and by the way, I'd just like to say what a fantastic Dad Dad is.'

'Did he pay you to say that?' asked Mum.

'No!' I protested. 'I really mean it. He's a brilliant Dad, totally awesome, so please don't leave him.'

'You weren't supposed to say that!' cried Dad.

Mum chuckled.

'I didn't tell him to say that,' said Dad.

'Just the other bit,' said Mum.

Dad was silent.

'I'm pleased you're writing a book together,' said Mum.

'And Thimble's staying,' I added.

'Thimble always was going to stay,' said Mum.

Dad was silent.

'Everything's perfect,' I said.

'I wouldn't quite go that far,' said Mum. She laughed, ruffled my hair, dropped back on the sofa and even gave Dad a little squeeze, which Dad might have enjoyed more if Thimble hadn't managed to get between them.

Just then – who'd have believed it – there was a knock at the doorbell.

'Not the Jehovah's Witnesses again!' groaned Dad.

'I'll get it,' I said.

I waltzed to the Great Door without a care in the world. But I was in for an unpleasant surprise.

The neighbours!

'Good evening,' said the man.

'We've come for our hamster,' said the woman.

I had to think fast. 'He's gone,' I blurted out.

'Gone?' asked the man. 'Gone where?'

'Abducted by aliens.'

The woman's face hardened. 'Now listen here,' she said. 'That hamster belongs to Billy Bunn's circus, and I have the certificate to prove it.' She flourished the said certificate in my face. I fumed.

'No one owns Thimble!' I said. 'He was born free, and lives here by his own free will!'

'I thought you said he'd been abducted by aliens,' said the man.

'You'd better let us in,' said the woman.

A tense stand-off ensued, ended by a hairy hand plucking the certificate from the woman's grasp and tearing it to pieces. All hell broke loose, with a screaming Thimble scurrying back into the castle, the neighbours chasing him, me chasing them, and Mum and Dad rushing in the other direction to see what was up.

Alas, it turned out that the neighbours were experts in martial arts. They employed the Nimzo-Indian Defence to repel Mum and Dad, then trapped Thimble underneath King Arthur's cocktail cabinet.

'Leave him alone!' I cried, but the woman neighbour issued a stern warning.

'Stay right where you are,' she said, 'or the hamster gets it.'

'What do you mean?'

The woman reached into her coat and drew out a sinister syringe. 'I am a trained vet,' she declared, 'and this is a powerful sedative. If there is no struggle, I will administer just enough to sedate the hamster. If, on the other hand … do you get my drift?'

We were in a hopeless situation.

'Get the monkey,' ordered the woman.

The man got down to the floor and

began inching under the cabinet. Thimble

gibbered fearfully.

Suddenly there was a cry from the man: 'What on earth?' He shot back from the cabinet, shaking his hand frantically. A great fat, hairy, eight-legged monster dropped to the floor and ran straight towards the woman.

'TARANTULA!' she screamed, dropping the syringe and legging it for all she was worth, closely followed by the man. Clearly in full attack mode, the tarantula chased them back out of the Great Hall, out of the West Door, away from the grounds of Dawson Castle, over the hills and far away, hopefully never to return.

'Now,' I declared, dusting myself down. 'Where were we?'

'I think we were saying that Thimble was going to stay,' said Mum.

'For ever and ever amen,' I replied.

Mum laughed, ruffled my hair, dropped back on the sofa and gave Thimble a little squeeze, which Thimble might have enjoyed more if Dad hadn't managed to get between them.

Dawson Castle had never felt more like home.